The butterfly maidens and the chrysalids love their beautiful gardens.

The chrysalids' baby brothers and sisters are called caterpillars. Their nursery is in the green meadow where Mother Silkmoth and Mother Swallowtail take care of them. They spin new gowns for the little caterpillars and make sure their bottles are filled with green leaf juice. When they get sleepy, the caterpillars nap in silken hammocks that swing gently between the trees.

First published in German in 1920 under the title *Im Schmetterlingsreich*
English version © Floris Books, Edinburgh 2009
British Library CIP Data available
ISBN 978-086315-688-5
Printed in China

Sibylle von Olfers

The Story of
the Butterfly Children

Floris Books

Far, far away from here the butterfly folk live in the Butterfly Kingdom. The little children are called chrysalids and they play joyfully in the beautiful gardens. The butterfly maidens watch over the chrysalids as they play and tell them all about the plants and pretty, brightly-coloured flowers. How wonderful they smell! The butterfly folk are very happy to have such fine gardens. How lucky they are!

The little caterpillars get up to all kinds of mischief!

Every afternoon the chrysalids go to Madam Dragonfly's dancing school. They learn how to dance among the flowers and balance on the thin stalks and grasses. Madam Dragonfly takes their hand and helps them to practice. One day they will all be as graceful and elegant as she is.

Oops! The chrysalids sometimes fall when they are learning to balance.

The first day of Spring is a very special day. The spring sun sends his messengers, the sunbeams, down to the Butterfly Kingdom and they present the chrysalids with their wings. How noble the sunbeams look in their golden robes and how brightly their golden lances shimmer. What an exciting day!

The
chrysalids
cannot wait
to get their
wings!

The cabbage white and brimstone butterflies are the first to receive their wings. They have learned all about the flowers and plants, and how to dance and weave among the stalks and grasses. They have done well! Together they flutter happily over the green meadows.

Higher and higher they fly through the mild spring air.

Soon all the other butterflies receive their wings and follow their friends into the air. They are not chrysalids any longer. They have become beautiful butterflies! The sky is full of colour as peacock, swallowtail, tortoiseshell, red admiral and many other butterflies dance and flutter all around. How happy they are to see each other.

The
butterflies stop
to rest on the
soft, white
flowers.

When night time comes, the moths have a long torchlight procession to celebrate this special day. They have received their wings too. The butterflies are all invited and the ones that have not already gone to bed join the moths and dance through the air with them. What a sight it is! They sing songs to welcome springtime and give thanks for their wings. The meadow flowers snoozing by the wayside are woken up by the gentle wing beats. They uncurl their petals and listen to the songs, and if you listen very carefully they'll tell you all about it!

On the first
day of Spring
you might hear
them too!

Sibylle von Olfers

Sibylle von Olfers' (1881–1916) blend of natural observation and use of simple design has led to comparisons with Kate Greenaway and Elsa Beskow.

She was born the third of five children in a castle in East Prussia. Encouraged by her aunt, she trained at art college. Her beauty attracted many admirers and suitors, but she remained aloof and distant from the "useless world of the aristocrats."

At the age of twenty-five she joined the Sisters of Saint Elizabeth, an order of nuns. As well as teaching art in the local school, she wrote and illustrated a number of children's books. Tragically she died at the age of thirty-four from a lung infection.

The Story of the Snow Children is her first book, published in 1905, followed by *The Story of the Root Children* (1906), *Princess in the Forest* (1909) and *The Story of the Wind Children* (1910).

The Story of
the Root-Children

Sibylle von Olfers

Floris Books

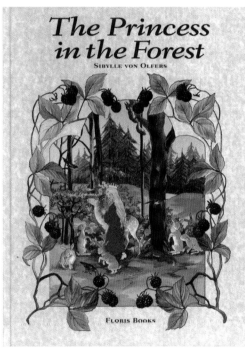

**The Princess
in the Forest**

SIBYLLE VON OLFERS

FLORIS BOOKS

The Story of the
Snow Children

Sibylle von Olfers

The
Story of the
Wind Children

Sibylle von Olfers